W9-AWJ-423

DISCARD

THE RUNAWAY FLYING HORSE

By PAUL JACQUES BONZON

Translated by Susan Kotta

Illustrated by WILLIAM PÈNE DU BOIS

PARENTS' MAGAZINE PRESS/NEW YORK

Originally "Le Petit Cheval de Bois" from Contes de l'Hiver
by P. J. Bonzon. Collection Anemones, Editions BIAS, Paris, 1960.
English translation copyright © 1976 by Parents' Magazine Press
Illustrations copyright © 1976 by William Pène du Bois
All rights reserved
Printed in the United States of America

Library of Congress Cataloging in Publication Data
Bonzon, Paul Jacques
  The runaway flying horse.
  Translation of Le petit cheval de bois.
  SUMMARY: Bored with his life on the merry-go-round,
a little wooden horse decides to run away.
  [1. Merry-go-round—Fiction] 1. Du Bois,
William Pène.   II. Title.
PZ7.B6447Ru   [E]   76-2525
ISBN 0-8193-0875-7   ISBN 0-8193-0876-5 lib. bdg.

To merry-go-rounds everywhere,
particularly to one in Watch Hill, Rhode Island,
where flying horses still whirl
round and round

From every corner of town, children came running. The merry-go-round had just opened for the season.

The merry-go-round! How beautiful they were, those little wooden horses with their shiny red leather saddles and gold bridles, their silky, real horsehair manes.

All things considered, they led a good life, those flying horses. Nothing to do but whirl round and round, carrying eager children to the merry music of a barrel organ.

But who in this world is ever satisfied? One of those little wooden horses grew bored. "How monotonous!" he sighed, "forever turning in circles to the same old tunes, with only children for riders."

Every day this little wooden horse saw, passing the carousel, car-
riages and wagons drawn by real horses. And he wanted to be a real
horse, too—one who could trot along the road and carry grown-up
passengers.

One night, while the other wooden horses were all sleeping peacefully under the merry-go-round's wooden canopy, he suddenly thought, "What if I should run away?"

It was a brave thought for a little wooden horse who had never stood by himself! He tried moving one foot. It would not budge. He tried another, then another, and finally the last. But his four hoofs remained suspended in midair.

In anger, he tried to rear up as he had once seen a real horse do. Unexpectedly—wonder of wonders!—he was free. It was so extraordinary, so marvelous to move about, that he could hardly believe his luck.

As quietly as he could, the little wooden horse slipped out from among his sleeping companions, thinking, "How stupid they are to settle for such a dull life." With a toss of his head, he jumped over the merry-go-round's gate and, in a single bound, into the road. No one saw him leave, for the entire town was asleep.

Clip-clop! Clip-clop! Alone through town, the little wooden horse went. Oh dear! The road was not nearly so soft as the breeze beneath his feet when the merry-go-round turned. His legs, quite stiff from being still for so long, did not hold him up very well either. And without the horseshoes real horses wear, his hoofs wore down as they scraped along the gravel. Never mind, he was free! He stopped and whinnied the way real horses do.

What fun!

Then he trotted on again. Clip-clop! Clip-clop! He continued in this way with a golden slice of moon above him in the sky. Then, tired out, he stopped by the side of the road. Suddenly, pricking up his ears, he heard a whinny just like his own.

"There must be real horses over there," thought the little wooden horse excitedly, "just like the ones by the merry-go-round!"

Following the sound, he trotted across the fields until he came to a large barn. The door was not quite shut, so he stepped inside.

"Phew!" he snorted. "What a disagreeable smell! I wonder if all the houses where real horses live smell this way." Picking his way daintily through the straw, he ventured farther into the stable. A big horse stood fast asleep. The little wooden horse came closer and tapped his foot to wake him. But so faint was the sound of his wooden hoof in straw that the big horse went right on sleeping.

Farther on, there stood a still bigger horse asleep, but he was so huge that the little wooden horse was frightened and shied away. Finally, in the last stall, a black horse was awake, watching him curiously.

"What do you want here?" she asked as the little wooden horse approached.

"I want to be a real horse."

"You—a mere merry-go-round horse?"

"I should like to have real iron shoes on my hoofs," the wooden horse went on, "and be able to pull people in a carriage—or do work in the fields that real horses do."

"Well," the black horse replied, not unkindly, "you will have to eat lots of hay and oats to grow big and strong. Men only like horses that are big and strong."

"Then I'll eat a lot and grow big and strong like you!" the little horse said happily. He had decided to stay in the stable.

And certainly he tried his best to eat lots of hay and oats, all summer long. But, alas, he had only a little wooden horse's stomach, and he hardly grew at all. After a while, he got tired of the rough stable life. The other horses made fun of him and his tiny hoofs without shoes, his red leather saddle and the shiny gold bridle which was beginning to tarnish. What's more, he could never get used to that awful smell the straw gave off. How much sweeter was the air at his own little merry-go-round! And that's how he came to miss the other wooden horses.

So one morning, tired of being laughed at, he left the stable and decided to go back to his friends. Clip-clop! Clip-clop! It was far, but luckily he remembered the road. It was lined with tall trees, and it ran along the seaside.

He came, at last, to the town.

Could it be?

The park he had left festooned with banners and full of music and happy children was now deserted. The green trees he remembered had turned brown. The merry-go-round was nowhere to be seen.

"How will I ever find my friends?" sighed the little horse.

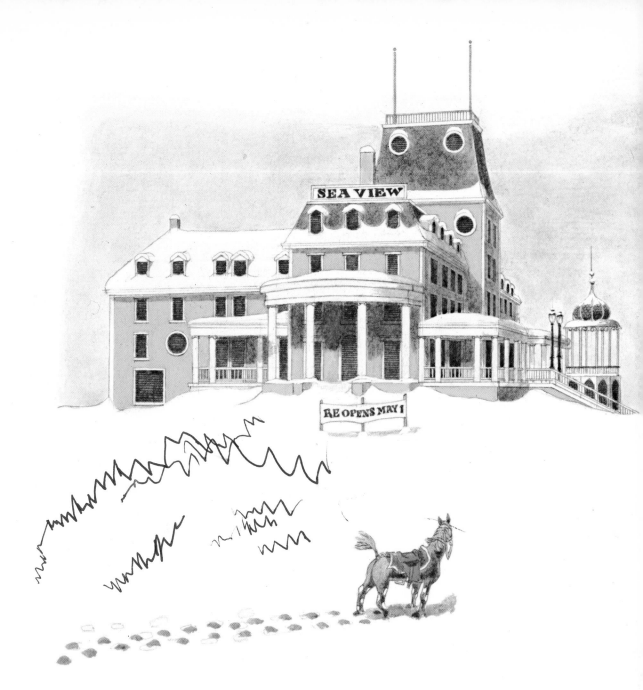

For weeks, he wandered the roads listening for the sweet sounds of the merry-go-round's barrel organ. Meanwhile the weather grew steadily colder and the rain turned to snow. Everything he saw had a quiet, strange look.

The chilly wind in the branches of bare trees made the only music to reach his ears.

CHEPLAIN'S TOYS AND GAMES

Then one day, he came to a much bigger town, with bright lights and shops lit up as though for a fair. Perhaps his merry-go-round would be here.

Soundlessly, the little wooden horse trotted along the snowy sidewalks. What beautiful shops! And they were filled with toys. It was a place made for just the sort of happy children he had once carried on his back. Soon, on the other side of a big glass wall, he thought he recognized his old friends. But what were they doing in there? Had they run away from the merry-go-round, too? He slipped quietly through the half-open door into the store.

"Hello, dear friends!" he said delightedly.

They looked with scorn at the little wooden horse. "We are no friends of yours. Look at your threadbare saddle, your frayed bridle, chipped paint and worn hoofs! We are brand new horses, not battered old wrecks."

"But you are not real horses," he said in confusion.

"We may not be real horses," they said haughtily, "but we are not merry-go-round horses either."

"Who are you, then?"

"Toys for the lucky children who will ask for us from Santa Claus."

At the word "children," the little wooden horse decided to stay. He jumped into the window beside the others.

Poor little horse! He expected some eager child to come along and pat his silky mane, or sit on his frayed leather saddle, as they once had done. Though lots of children pressed their noses to the glass wall every day and pointed out the horses to their mothers and fathers, he was never chosen.

"Why don't they want me?" he asked the others.

"You have no rockers to rock on," they said proudly, "or wheels to roll on, as we do. They'll never want a tired old horse like you!"

The little wooden horse grew sadder and sadder, but still he hoped that a finger would point his way. Alas! one morning he awoke to find the shop less brightly lit. No children came by at all.

"What's happening?" he asked.

"Don't you know?" scoffed a donkey who had not been chosen either. "Christmas is over. Finished and done for this year. And you and I won't be going down any chimneys. Pretty soon, the store-keeper will move us upstairs, into the loft. Then he'll throw an old canvas over us to keep out the dust—until next Christmas."

"Never!" the little wooden horse shuddered. And when nighttime came, he jumped through the glass door—and out of the store—to continue his search for the merry-go-round.

Clip-clop! Clip-clop! Once again, and for weeks on end, he roamed over the icy roads, through biting winds. His leather saddle was worn to shreds, his paint all chipped and peeling.

Finally, in despair, he went back to the very town where his merry-go-round had once been. And there—in the park—he saw it again! Instantly, he recognized the smiling faces of children painted on its top.

With a bound, he leapt over the gate to find his old place in the second row, next to the music. But what a shock! His spot had been taken by another horse.

All his little wooden horse courage left him. He had come so far, and they had forgotten him. Not for the world could he bring himself to take to the road again. He wanted neither to be back in the stable with the real horses, nor in the loft where the Christmas toys lay covered with canvas. What was the good of going on if the carousel had no room for him anymore? All hope now lost, he simply collapsed.

There was a great clatter as he fell. And a man's voice called out, "Hey, look here! We've forgotten one last horse. He's even missed out on his new spring painting."

And before the little wooden horse knew what was happening, the worker had lifted him off the floor and was repainting him a beautiful caramel color. He gave him a lovely golden mane and new red saddle and shiny bridle, too.

Then—miracle of miracles—a place was found for him in the second row, after all. Right by the music! The little wooden horse nearly burst with joy. And, as you can imagine, there he has stayed, content to this day.